BIG
YELLOW
DIGGER

To George, Mia, Cameron, Sam and Ben — J.J.

For Freyja Björk — A.R.

ORCHARD BOOKS

First published in Great Britain in 2011 by Orchard Books
This edition published in 2016 by The Watts Publishing Group

1 3 5 7 9 10 8 6 4 2

Text © Julia Jarman, 2011

Illustrations © Adrian Reynolds, 2011

A CIP catalogue record for this book is available from the British Library.

ISBN 978 1 40834 677 8

Printed and bound in China

Orchard Books

An imprint of

Hachette Children's Group

Part of The Watts Publishing Group Limited

Carmelite House, 50 Victoria Embankment, London EC4Y 0DZ

Hachette Ireland, 8 Castlecourt, Castleknock, Dublin 15, Ireland

An Hachette UK Company

www.hachette.co.uk

www.hachettechildrens.co.uk

JULIA JARMAN & ADRIAN REYNOLDS

BIG YELLOW DIGGER

ORCHARD

Ben and Bella on the big yellow digger —

Brum brum!
Brum brum!
Judder,
judder,
jigger.

Bucket goes up.
Bucket goes down.
Digger's big tracks
go rolling round.

But who's that standing by the tree?

"Hello, kids, is there room for me?"
"'Course there is, Moose! We'll help you.
You can ride in the digger, too."

Moose climbs in with help from Ben.
The big yellow digger rolls on again.

Moose, Ben and Bella on the big yellow digger —

Brum brum!
Brum brum!
Judder, judder, jigger.

Bucket goes up.
Bucket goes down.
Digger is racing over the ground.

But who's that racing after us?

"It's Zebra and Rhinoceros!"
"Hi there, kids, can we have a ride?"
"'Course you can, boys, just climb inside!"

Zebra climbs up — and so does Mole! —
Rhino roars, "Let's dig a hole!"

Moose, Zebra and Rhino,
Ben and Bella in the digger —
and Mole — and Duck! —
"Our hole is getting BIGGER!"

Bucket goes

down,

down,

down,

down.

"We're making a tunnel under the ground!
But stop! What is that wailing sound?"

"Help! Help!" The wail grows wailier.
"Please take me back to Australia!
I must be home in time for tea
because my mummy's missing me."

"It's Little Roo. Be our guest!
Jump up, Roo! We'll do our best."

Moose, Zebra and Rhino, Ben and Bella in the digger –

Mole, Duck and Roo,
Judder, judder, jigger.

Digger's tracks go rolling round,

deeper and deeper under the ground.

But stop! — there's a . . . .

dinosaur.

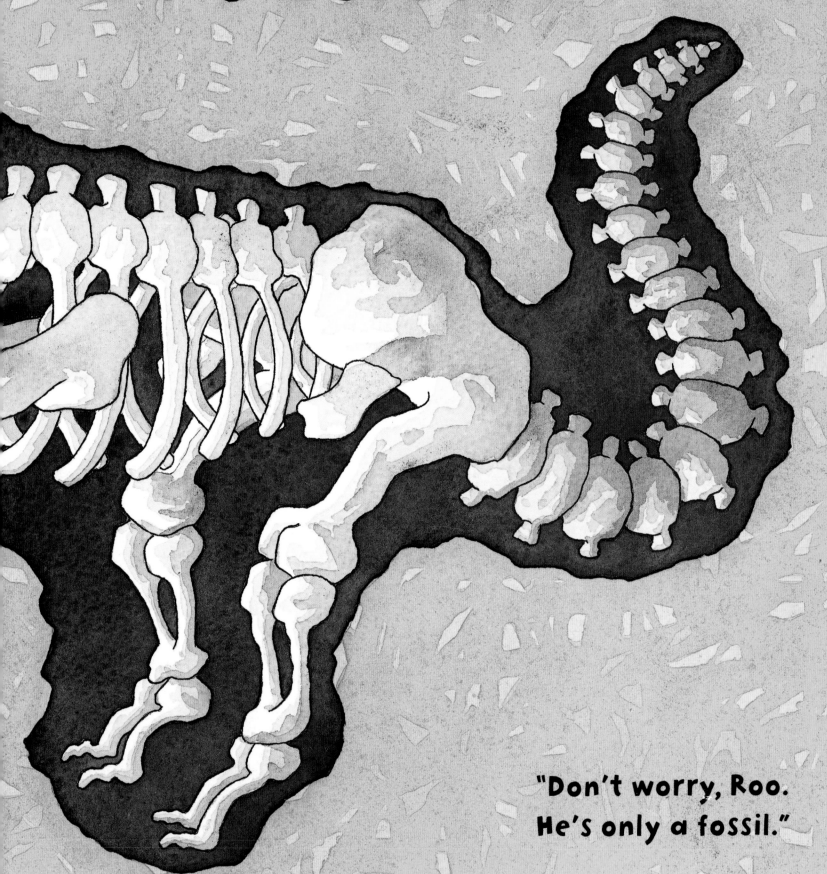

Digger swerves past. We're in a hurry.
Got to get Little Roo back to his mummy.
"What a rollicking, roaring ride!
And look — we've reached the other side!"

Who's that peering down at us?

Wombat, Possum and Platypus.
"Hello, Little Roo!
Do you want your mummy?"

But Roo's on his way
to the pouch in her tummy!

Digger rolls out. "We're here, yippee!"
Kanga cooks a barbie for their tea.

They dance to Wombat's didgeridoo.
They play boomerang with Little Roo.

They make dotty pictures in the sand.

They swing with Possum by one hand.

Then Rhino shouts, "Kids, come on!
Your mum's wondering where
    you've gone.
Say goodbye to your Aussie mates.
Hurry, hurry, it's getting late!"

Brum brum! Brum brum!
Judder, judder, jigger.
All aboard the **big yellow digger!**

Bucket goes up.
Bucket goes down,
Here we go again — under the ground.

Deep into the earth, dark as night.
Quickly, Bella, turn on the lights!

Wow! Aren't we going fast?

Wave to the dino as we whizz past.

Here's the end of our very big hole.
Wave goodbye to Duck and Mole.